FLAT STANLEY

The Fire Station

EGMONT

We bring stories to life

Book Band: Gold

First published in Great Britain 2012
This Reading Ladder edition published 2016
by Egmont UK Limited
The Yellow Building, 1 Nicholas Road, London W11 4AN

Illustrations by Jon Mitchel
The author and illustrator have asserted their moral rights
ISBN 978 1 4052 8209 3
www.egmont.co.uk
A CIP catalogue record for this title is available from the British Library.
Printed in Singapore
47004/4

Series consultant: Nikki Gamble

FLAT STANLEY

The Fire Station

Written by Lori Haskins Houran Illustrations by Jon Mitchell

Based on the original character created by Jeff Brown

Reading Ladder

Stanley Lambchop lived with his mother, his father and his little brother, Arthur.

Stanley was four feet tall, about
a foot wide, and half an inch thick.
He had been flat ever since a bulletin
board fell on him.

Stanley's family found it handy
having a flat boy at home,
and Stanley didn't mind helping out.

Stanley held tools for his father
while Mr Lambchop repaired the car.

He helped Arthur
practise his backflips.

Stanley gave Mrs Lambchop
a perfect place to roll out pastry,
except when he felt ticklish.

It turned out that Stanley made an excellent stencil, too.

'Hold still,' said Arthur.

Stanley held his breath as Arthur traced him carefully.

Children all over the city
were entering a poster contest
for Fire Safety Month.

‘I hope we win the trip to the fire station!’ said Arthur.

‘Me, too,’ said Stanley. ‘I’ve always wanted to slide down the pole.’

The next Monday, a letter arrived.

'Hey, guess what?' shouted Arthur.

'Hay is for horses,' Mrs Lambchop said.

'Try to remember that, dear.'

‘Sorry,’ said Arthur. ‘Guess what? Our poster won the contest. We’re going to the fire station on Saturday!’

Mrs Lambchop clapped.

'I knew you boys had my talent for art,' she said proudly.

Stanley and Arthur practised
fire drills all week long.
Arthur crawled around the house
on his hands and knees.

Stanley did the Stop, Drop and Roll.

(Mostly the Roll.)

At last, Saturday came.

The Lambchops drove to the fire station.

'Welcome!' bellowed Chief Abbot.

A puppy bounced at his feet.

'ARF ARF ARF ARF ARF!'

'Don't mind Spark,' said the Chief.

'He's still in training!'

Chief Abbot led the Lambchops through the fire station kitchen. 'We firefighters cook up some tasty meals,' he said.

Mr Lambchop got out his camera.

He took a picture of a pot of chilli.

Everyone went on to the bunk room.

'Very nice,' said Mrs Lambchop.

'Can I see the fire engines?' said Arthur.

'Of course!' said Chief Abbot.

He led everyone down to the garage.

Stanley was disappointed.

He had wanted to get there by pole.

Boots and trousers lay on the floor.

'Oh my,' said Mrs Lambchop.

I could tidy up if you'd like.'

Chief Abbot laughed.

'We leave these out so we can jump into them in an emergency,' he said.

'Neat!' said Stanley.

Chief Abbot pointed at a fire engine.

'Climb on up if you like.'

'Wow!' said Arthur.

The boys scrambled on to the fire engine.

Spark was right behind them.

I want to drive it!

Suddenly, the alarm bell rang.
'Chief, Code Nine on Oak Street,'
called a firefighter.

The Chief turned to the Lambchops.

'How would you folks like

to come along on a rescue?'

'A rescue? Will it be safe?'

asked Mr Lambchop.

'You bet!' said Chief Abbot.

'Code Nine means a cat up a tree.

Probably Furball again.'

Mr Lambchop looked at his wife.

She gave a little nod.

'YES!' yelled Stanley and Arthur.

'Stanley, turn on the siren! Arthur, hit the lights!' shouted Chief Abbot.

'My goodness, is that necessary?' asked Mrs Lambchop.

'No,' said Chief Abbot. 'It's just more fun this way!'

The fire engine raced through the city.

Soon it pulled up to a tall tree.

A tiny cat shivered at the top.

Meow!

'She's pretty high up this time,' said Chief Abbot.

Spark panted at the chief's feet.

'All right. Let's get her down.'

Two firefighters raised the ladder.

The Lambchops moved out of the way.

Chief Abbot climbed until Furball was just a few feet away.
'Good kitty,' he said, stretching out his hands.
'Come here, Furball.'

The cat got ready to leap into
the Chief's arms.
Just then, Spark started to bark.
'ARF ARF ARF ARF ARF!'

For a second, Furball froze.

Then she jumped the other way.

'Furball!' cried Chief Abbot.

He was too late.

Furball was heading for the ground!

The Lambchops looked up.

Their mouths were open in surprise.

All at once, Stanley threw himself on to the grass.

'Grab my hands!' he told his mother.

Mrs Lambchop grabbed his hands.

'Grab my feet!' he told Arthur.

But Arthur didn't move.

‘HEY!’ shouted Mrs Lambchop at the top of her lungs. ‘GRAB HIS FEET!’

Arthur blinked.

He grabbed Stanley’s feet.

‘Stretch!’ cried Stanley.

Arthur and Mrs Lambchop stretched Stanley between them. They were not a second too soon.

Boing! Meow!

Furball bounced twice on Stanley's belly, then landed safely on the ground.

The firefighters started clapping.

Arthur and Mrs Lambchop stood Stanley back up.

Arthur looked at his mother.

'Hay is for horses,' he said.

'Remember?'

Mrs Lambchop grinned.

'Good work, Lambchops!'

said Chief Abbot, racing over.

'How can we ever thank you?'

'Well,' said Stanley.

'There is one thing . . .'

'WHEEEEEEE!'